D0007897

Stone Arch Books
a Capstone Imprint

Benji Franklin: Kid Zillionaire
is published by Stone Arch Books,
a Capstone Imprint
1710 Roe Crest Drive
North Mankato, Minnesota 56003
www.capstonepub.com

Cataloging-in-Publication Data is available on
the Library of Congress website.
ISBN: 978-1-4342-6418-3 (library hardcover)

Summary: After inventing a best-selling computer app,
Benjamin "Benji" Franklin becomes a ZILLIONAIRE! This
twelve-year-old tycoon has the world in the palm of his
hand. But when a meteor threatens Earth, Benji will need
all his riches (and a superpowered rocket ship) to save the
planet from certain doom!

Graphic Designer: Brann Garvey
Creative Director: Heather Kindseth
Production Specialist: Laura Manthe

APR 1 7 2014

Printed in the United States of America in Stevens Point, Wisconsin
092013   007765WZS14

BENJI FRANKLIN

FRANKLIN

KID ZILLIONAIRE

BUILDING WEALTH

(and Superpowered Rockets!)

written by
Raymond Bean

illustrated by
Matthew Vimislik

Table of Contents

Introduction 6

CHAPTER 1
Asteroids! 8

CHAPTER 2
Big Trouble 16

CHAPTER 3
Spacing Out 24

CHAPTER 4
Riding in Style 31

CHAPTER 5
Up, Up, and Away 38

CHAPTER 6
The Asteroid Net 45

CHAPTER 7
Suit Up! 54

CHAPTER 8
Zero Gravity 65

CHAPTER 9
Nice Catch! 70

CHAPTER 10
Bright Future 78

Introduction

My name's Benji Franklin! After inventing a best-selling computer app that helps people come up with creative and time-saving excuses, I became the world's youngest and, well, only ZILLIONAIRE!

But I quickly discovered that life wasn't all about the Benjamins. I've decided to use my newfound wealth for the greater good—like saving the world from cloned killer dinosaurs, building super-powered rocket ships, and launching a solid gold submarine. Or two!

Here's a few people you should know:

DAD: He likes building one-of-a-kind inventions, and he spends a lot of time tinkering in our workshop. His latest projects include an orbiting surveillance satellite and magnet suits that can rescue drowning sailors. Plus, he's always excited about my ideas!

MOM: She's always putting other people before herself. She is a regular volunteer at the food shelf and taught me that helping others is important, rewarding, and fun. She also runs a farm (which I bought her).

PROFESSOR SNOW: He knows everything there is to know about cloning, climate change, nano-bots, and anything else that can easily turn into a catastrophe. I recently helped him save the world from Troodon dinosaurs!

That's about it.

Okay, time to save the world...again!

CHAPTER 1
Asteroids!

One morning, I was out in the workshop downloading data from the satellite. Dad was working on his magnetic suits. He'd reversed the magnets and his safety system seemed about ready for a real-life trial. He had a fisherman in town that agreed to try it out with his crew. He'd dropped his boat off at our workshop earlier in the morning, and Dad was installing the system in the boat.

That's when I saw it...

An asteroid appeared on the satellite's data system. It was on course to collide with Earth!

"You might want to take a look at this, Dad," I said, my heart pounding.

He was under the boat, twisting at something with his wrench. "I can't right now, Benji. Is it good news or bad?" he asked.

"Both," I said.

"Well, does it look like something's going to take out our satellite?" he asked.

"Well, no, and that's part of the good news," I told him. "The bad news...this might take out the planet. The WHOLE planet!!"

My dad is super organized. Everything he owns has a place, and he always puts things where they belong. I thought it was kind of funny that even though there was an asteroid screaming toward the planet, the first thing he did was put his wrench carefully back in his toolbox. If there was a time to simply drop it on the floor and be sloppy, this was it!

"What's the other good news?" asked Dad.

"Maybe we can stop it," I said.

"Benji, this asteroid is rushing toward Earth at incredible speed. I don't think we can do anything," he said, skeptical.

"From my calculations, the asteroid is still sixty days from impact," I explained.

"Then I wouldn't panic just yet," he said. "I've seen space debris that looked like it was on course for impact suddenly change direction and sail right on by. Now, it's getting late. You need to get to the bus stop."

Huh?!? How can he expect me to go to school after what I just told him? "I don't think you heard me when I screamed, 'the WHOLE planet,'" I said. "I need to track this asteroid and send the data to someone who can help save us! Then maybe I can buy a laser canon...or a supersized missile launcher...or a titanium flyswatter the size of a football field, or—"

"Benji, you're in sixth grade," he said. "The world can survive without you on this one. You're not the only person with a satellite tracking this thing. Everything will be fine."

Obviously, I didn't agree, but I could tell there was no way Dad was going to let me stay home.

$ $ $

On the ride to school, all I could think about was the asteroid. I was working on my smartphone, which was really hard to do with the bus bouncing and all the kids talking. I made a list of the ways to destroy or send an asteroid off course:

HOW TO STOP THE ASTEROID

1. **Blow to bits.**
2. **Send off course with mega-ton explosion.**
3. **Redirect course with giant sail.**
4. **Jackhammer to pieces with high-tech machines.**
5. **Create a chemical reaction to disintegrate.**

I was so focused on my list that I didn't notice this person sitting next to me. Cindy Meyers. "You know, you're not allowed to use your smartphone on the bus," she said. "You think just because your app is so popular that you can do whatever you want?"

I rolled my eyes. "Good morning to you, too, Cindy," I said, trying to be polite. "I'm busy on an important project. It's not like I'm playing video games or texting like you."

"I'm not texting or talking on my phone because that would be against school rules," she whined.

"I'll be watching," I said, getting back to work.

"That makes two of us," she warned. "It's going to be a real shame when the principal takes your smartphone away and bans you from the bus."

"If you knew what I was working on you wouldn't be giving me a hard time," I said.

She laughed. "I find that hard to believe."

Cindy had always been difficult, but she was being extra annoying today.

"What's your problem?" I asked.

"I don't have a problem," she said. "You're the one who thinks you're so cool ever since you created that ridiculous Excuse Yourself app."

"Who said I think I'm cool?" I said. "For your information, I've never been considered cool."

"Well, you don't act like it. You created that app, and then you didn't even have to come to school because you're a big shot now. You weren't the only one who worked hard on that app project," she said.

She was upset that her app didn't get more attention than mine. I couldn't even remember what her app did! "I haven't been to school because I was busy helping out the food shelter," I explained.

"I think you're a troublemaker," she said.

"Then why'd you sit next to me?" I asked. I had bigger things to think about than Cindy.

"Because I'm on the School Decency Committee and you're on my radar," Cindy explained. "You haven't been around to see the damage your app created. Kids are making up all kinds of excuses for things thanks to your reckless idea."

I got a little anxious because I had barely been to school since I created the app. I knew tons of people had downloaded it, but I hadn't had any time to see how kids were using it.

"Well," I began, "I'm about to see for myself."

CHAPTER 2
Big Trouble

Everything seemed pretty much the same as usual when I got to school. My app wasn't causing any problems as far as I could see. I was definitely getting more attention than usual though. More people seemed to know my name, which was funny because before the app I wasn't exactly popular.

On my way to tech class, a few kids patted me on the back. I didn't like all the attention. It was a little stressful. I found myself walking quicker than usual. I slipped into my seat in tech class, relieved to be out of the hall.

The teacher started the lesson by welcoming me back to school. The class erupted with applause. "You're a superstar these days," she said. "We've been following your success online. I can't believe how huge your app, Excuse Yourself, has become."

I'd been so busy with the Troodon dinosaurs and Dr. Snow that I hadn't had time to read what was being said about the app.

"I'm pretty shocked myself," I said. "Honestly, I haven't been able to follow what's going on with the app because I've been working."

"I thought you were out because of the app," Mrs. Heart said curiously.

"Actually, I was busy with another project for my mom's food pantry," I explained. "The principal, Mrs. Petty, gave me permission to take a few days to work on it. Remember?"

"That's not an excuse, is it?" Mrs. Heart joked.

"No, but maybe I should add it to the app," I said with a smile.

"Are you rich?" said a student in the back.

"It's not polite to ask someone a question like that," said Mrs. Heart. "We're all very happy for you though, Benji."

Realizing that everyone at school knew I made a TON of money was kind of embarrassing. James, the kid sitting next to me, leaned over and whispered, "How much do you actually have?"

"I don't know," I said, which was basically the truth because the number was always changing. I'd checked the total before school, but there were too many zeros to count!

CHA-CHING! CHA-CHING!!

I'd only been out of school for a week, but it felt like a year.

$ $ $

When I got home later that day, I went straight to the workshop. Dad was at the computer and looked like he'd been there all day.

"Benji, I was wrong," he said. "People don't seem to be tracking this thing. You've found something that others haven't noticed yet. I can see why! It's not a known asteroid. I've been searching the database all day and can't find any record of it."

"What does that mean?" I asked.

"We might be the only ones who know it's there," he exclaimed. "Most satellites are designed to locate asteroids larger than a kilometer. My satellite is great at detecting asteroids *smaller* than a kilometer. This one is about the size of a twenty-story building, so it's much harder to locate than a larger one."

I did the math in my head. A story on a building is about twelve feet high. If the asteroid was twenty stories, it measured about 240 feet long!

"That's small?" I asked.

"Compared to some larger asteroids," said Dad. "It's big enough to cause a lot of damage, but still small enough to go undetected. The good news is it won't destroy the planet, but if it hits it will do some real damage."

"Shouldn't we call someone or notify the government?" I asked.

"Not yet," he said. "Let's give it a few days and see if it changes course. We have some time."

I logged on to my computer to research the kind of damage an asteroid would do if it impacted Earth. I learned that the asteroid that caused the extinction of the dinosaurs was about six miles wide.

The asteroid I located wasn't even close to the size of that one, but it was large enough to level buildings for five miles from the impact location.

I worked to try and calculate the impact date. I knew Dad was doing the same.

ASTEROIDS

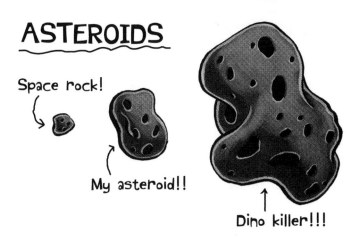

Space rock!

My asteroid!!

Dino killer!!!

Neither one of us said anything for about an hour. Then, I broke the silence.

"If my calculations are correct," I said. "The asteroid will hit Earth on Mom's birthday!"

I didn't have the heart to tell Mom that the world could be blasted by an asteroid on her birthday. When I went out to the farm later that night, I didn't say anything about it.

Mom hadn't wasted any time taking over the farm I'd recently bought her. It was already producing milk and eggs, and she had a full-time staff. She also bought a few refrigerated trucks for deliveries. That night, she was checking on the chickens, as I walked alongside her.

"You've been on your computer too long again," she said. "Your eyes are all bloodshot."

"No more than usual," I said.

She stopped and took another look at me. "What's on your mind, Benji? You look troubled."

"I'm fine, Mom. Today was my first day back to school. It was a little strange. Kids are really focused on the app and all the money I'm making." I said this knowing it was partially true, and my real concern was the asteroid.

"Kids your age don't normally experience this kind of success," she said. "It's natural for your friends to be confused and ask a lot of questions."

"I guess," I replied.

"There's something else that you're not telling me," she said. "What is it?"

I couldn't lie to my mother. "Our satellite located an asteroid this morning. It's on track to smash Earth in about a month."

"I know. Your father told me a few hours ago," she said, walking ahead of me.

"WHAT?! Why didn't you tell me that?"

"I wanted to see if you'd tell me on your own. Why didn't you tell me?" she said.

"I didn't want to worry you," I explained.

"I'm not worried, Benji."

"You should be!" I exclaimed. "It's on a collision course with the planet. The WHOLE planet!"

"You'll figure something out," she suggested.

Mothers. They're always so supportive. But this problem was a little out of my league.

"I bet you already have a solution brewing inside that head, and you don't even know it yet," she said. "You don't want an asteroid ruining your mother's birthday, do you?"

CHAPTER 3

Spacing Out

I went for a walk by myself on the trails behind the farm. I couldn't help feeling that a Troodon was going to jump out at me from behind a tree.

It was pretty surreal when I stopped to think about how much things had changed in such a short time. It was hard to even remember a time before Excuse Yourself.

As I walked, I imagined scenarios that might change the course of the asteroid or destroy it. I'd read online once that if you blow up the asteroid it becomes a bunch of small asteroids instead of one big one. The group of smaller ones acts like a shotgun blast and can cause even more damage!

My mind kept cycling through all the scenarios I'd listed on my computer. There simply had to be a solution.

Instead of blowing up the asteroid, what if there was a way to capture it? I wondered. I could land some sort of remote-control unit on it and simply fly it like a spaceship.

I tripped on a large stone and stopped to pick it up. I held it in my hands for a while wondering how I could stop it if it were hurtling through space at thousands of miles per hour.

I threw it as hard as I could and watched it sail into the woods. I picked up another stone and hurled it the same direction. A vision of a net wrapping around the stone came to me.

A net would stop or slow the stone down, but I couldn't figure out how to get a large net into space. Even if I did, could I could change the course of an asteroid?

I picked up another stone, and my phone rang.

"Hey, Dad," I answered.

"Hi, Benji," he said. "I just spoke with Dr. Snow. He has someone he'd like you to meet."

"The Troodon didn't escape again, did they?" I asked, hoping that wasn't the case.

"Nope, the dinos are safe and sound," Dad said. "This is about the asteroid. Why don't you have Mom drive you home? We need to talk."

$ $ $

When I got home, Dad was sifting through old airplane parts in the back field. "What's up?" I asked.

He climbed out from the rusted cockpit of a small plane and sat on the wing. "Come on over," he said, dusting off a place for me to sit.

"What are you doing?" I asked.

"I'm looking for spare parts to see if I can make another low-orbit rocket," he said, "but I wanted you to come home to talk about Dr. Snow."

"What did he say?" I asked.

"He asked my permission to give our number to another scientist," he explained.

"Why?" I asked.

"He said he wasn't sure, but that a very prominent scientist contacted him for help, and he suggested you."

"What did you say?"

"That between the Troodon and Excuse Yourself you've been busy," said Dad. "It might be good to take a little break."

"I'm fine, Dad," I assured him. "I'm too rich to take a break."

Just then, my phone rang.

"Hello," I said.

From the other side, in an English accent, a man's voice said, "Hello, Benjamin. My name is Sir Robert Dransling. You come highly recommended by Dr. Snow."

"That was fast," I said.

"There's no time to waste," he replied. "A situation has come to my attention in the past twenty-four hours that causes me great concern. If my information is correct, you've noticed this—ahem—problem as well."

"You mean the asteroid?" I asked.

"SHHHHH!" he said. "Someone might hear you. If people learn there's an asteroid on a collision course with the planet, they will go completely loopy. Discretion is the best course, lad. We mustn't breathe a word of this to anyone else."

I looked around at the back field, the rusty plane, and Dad. "My lips are sealed," I said.

"I'll send for you tomorrow," he said. "I'm flying you out to New Mexico so we can talk in person."

"But I have school tomorrow—"

"I'll see you tomorrow, Mr. Franklin. There's not a moment to waste." Then he hung up.

"He wants me in New Mexico tomorrow," I said.

"You have school," said Dad, "and I'm doing my first test of the magnetic system out at sea."

"We'll figure something out," I told Dad.

"Who was that man anyway?" he asked.

"He said his name was Sir Robert Dransling," I replied.

"Sir Robert Dransling?!" Dad exclaimed. "He's a world leader in space technology. They say he'll be the first person to provide space flights to tourists as a vacation!"

Really? I thought. *Maybe he can help me with my space station zoo idea!*

CHAPTER 4

Riding in Style

I went to school the next day like any other day. The phone rang in my math class. My teacher answered and then told me to head down to the office because I was going home early.

The secretary at the front desk and Mrs. Petty, the principal, looked confused.

"Benji, your father called and told us to release you early," Mrs. Petty said.

I looked around the room. "Who's picking me up?" I asked.

The secretary pointed outside. Through the window, I could see a long black limousine parked in front of the school. Its windows were tinted, and there was a tiny British flag painted on the passenger door.

"What's that?" I asked.

"We were hoping you could tell us," said the principal. "It's highly unusual for a student to be picked up by a non-family member."

"Who's in the limo?" I asked.

"Your father wouldn't say," she told me. "He just said that he was out at sea and your mother was out of town on business for the pantry and that a limo would be by to pick you up."

"All right then," I said. "I'm free to go?"

"Yes, I hope everything is fine," Mrs. Petty said.

When she said, "I hope everything is fine," I realized that she thought something was wrong. Based on her expression, she probably thought someone in my family had died or something.

"Everything is fine," I said.

"Keep up that positive attitude," Mrs. Petty said.

When I walked out, a man stepped out of the driver's seat and opened the back door. I realized that all the classes facing the front of the building were full of kids pressed up against the windows.

"Good morning, Mr. Franklin," the chauffeur said in a British accent.

"Nice car," I said. I wasn't sure what else to say to him. My heart was racing pretty fast.

"I realize this is highly unusual," he said. "However, we are in the midst of a decidedly unusual circumstance. Your father is returning from the fishing vessel he's on, and he asked us to pick you up in order to save time. I have your mother on a live video chat."

He held out his phone, and I could see Mom on the screen. "Hi, Benji," she said. "I'm already on the road and your father is on the boat. Sir Robert sent this car for you. It's going to take you to meet Dad at the dock, and then you're off."

"Off to where?" I asked.

"Your father has all the details," she said. "I wish I could tag along, but I'm halfway to Shiny Desert to make my delivery."

"Okay, Mom," I said. "Does this mean I'll be out of school for a few days?"

"I don't know, honey," she said.

The chauffeur nodded his head to indicate that I would in fact be out for a few days. I gave him a thumbs-up.

"You've already missed too many days," said Mom. "I don't want you missing too much more. But, this seems like the opportunity of a lifetime, and I'll let your father decide. He'll be with you the whole time. Have fun, and give me a call later to let me know how things are going."

$ $ $

During the ride to pick up Dad, the driver kept the glass wall between the front seat and the back of the limo shut. It was a little strange sitting alone in the back of that huge car. I ate a few bags of peanuts and watched some television.

I may have to buy one of these, I thought. *And maybe one for Mom, too. Then she wouldn't have to drive herself to places like Shiny Desert all alone.*

Dad hopped in when we reached the docks. He was wearing one of his magnetic fisherman suits.

"How is the suit working?" I asked.

"Really well," he said. "But we've only tested it in calm water. I'll have to increase the magnetic force on the boat for it to work correctly in rough seas."

I was wondering how long it was going to take Dad to acknowledge that I was out of school on a weekday. And that we were being driven in a limo by a complete stranger.

"Sounds great," I said. "Anything else going on?"

"Not really," he replied.

I watched him checking out the TV for a while until he finally snapped out it. "What's the deal? Where are we going?" he asked.

"Are you going to wear that magnetic suit the whole time?" I said.

Dad quickly unscrewed his helmet. "Where are we going, Benji?"

"I thought you knew," I said.

The glass partition between the front and back seat suddenly slid down. The chauffeur glanced toward us over his shoulder. "We're driving to the airport," he said.

"But where are we going?" I said.

"The desert," he told us.

"Desert?" cried Dad. "Which one? Besides, I'm not dressed for the desert!"

The glass wall smoothly slid upward and cut us off again from the driver.

"How many deserts are in New Mexico?" I asked.

The rest of the ride Dad told me all about Sir Robert Dransling. He sounded like a wildly successful guy. He owned newspapers, shipping businesses, TV stations, radio stations, and a ton of technology companies. He'd even been knighted by the Queen of England!

Why did he need me?

CHAPTER 5

Up, Up, and Away

We drove up to a special gate at the airport. Security guards opened it, and we drove right onto the runway. It was a special section of the airport for all the private jets.

"Wow!" Dad said. He's been a plane nut ever since he was a kid.

I lowered the divider between the driver and us. "Are we going on one of these jets?" I asked.

"The one at the end," he said.

At the end of all the amazing jets was the coolest one of all. It looked like a bullet with wings.

"That's the ECS Bolt 41," Dad said.

"I see you know your aircraft," the driver said. "But that's actually the ECS Bolt 42. It's *next* year's model. No one else has anything like it."

"It looks like half plane, half space ship," I said.

"You could say that. Ah, we are here," he said, stopping the car. He climbed out and politely opened my door.

Dad and I stepped out.

A long staircase slowly lowered from the plane. A man stood at the top. He waved.

"That's Sir Robert Dransling," whispered Dad.

Sir Robert was super tan, like he'd been in the sun every day of his life. I was surprised he wasn't in a business suit or at least dressed up a little. He wore flip-flops and one of those brightly colored Hawaiian shirts.

He shook my hand. "Mr. Franklin, please climb aboard and make yourself at home," he said.

I'd been on a plane two other times in my life: once to Florida and once to California. On both of those trips, we flew on a regular plane.

This plane was straight out of a movie.

The luxury aircraft looked like an expensive hotel. There were actual rooms. It had a living room, kitchen, and even a few bedrooms.

"Can I get you gentlemen something to eat?" asked Sir Robert.

"We'd love a few turkey sandwiches, if it's not too much trouble," Dad said. "I've been out on the water all morning, and Benjamin didn't have a chance to eat lunch yet."

Sir Robert pressed a button on his phone. "Done," he said. "They will be out in a few minutes."

"That's pretty cool," I said.

"I agree," he said. "It's very cool. From what I hear about you, young Benjamin, you could buy a plane like this of your own."

"Maybe I will," I said.

"I didn't make my first million until I was twenty-five," said Sir Robert. "From what I understand, you're only twelve, and you're way beyond that."

"Benjamin hasn't had a whole lot of time to really think about the money he's made," my dad explained. "He's been busy working for Dr. Snow since the app was released."

"I've also been helping my mother establish a small farm for the food pantry she runs," I added.

"Intelligent, modest, and giving. You might just be my new favorite person, young Benji," Sir Robert said.

Just then, a waiter handed me a plate with a turkey sandwich and a soda.

"And you might be mine," I said, smiling and raising my glass.

"I can offer you much more than a simple sandwich, Benji," said Sir Robert. "I contacted you because I know that you have a low-orbit satellite collecting data on space debris. I have several of my own in orbit. My team and I first spotted the asteroid a few days ago. I realized that you and I were probably the only two people with satellites designed to identify an asteroid of that size."

"It was very cool of you to invite us here," I said. "But what exactly can we do for you?"

"It's what I think we may be able to accomplish together," he replied. "My focus in life is on helping others reach their full potential. I'm sure my team could figure out some way to deflect or destroy this asteroid, but I'm more interested in what *you* would do with it, Benji."

"Since you're so wealthy, don't you have access to the world's best scientists?" I asked. "Why are you asking me?"

"Indeed I do have access to the world's best and brightest," he said. "However, as I've already pointed out, you seem to be the only other person to spot the asteroid. If the 'world's best scientists' haven't even been able to locate the asteroid, why would I want their help in trying to destroy it?"

I thought about what he said for a moment. It was kind of amazing that no one else had detected an asteroid that could possibly level cities and towns if nothing was done to change its course.

"The reason I asked you here is that I believe you're an extraordinary young man," Sir Robert continued. "I told Dr. Snow that having those Troodon was going to become a problem. What surprised me was when he told me a twelve-year-old solved the problem for him. I'd like to know what you'd do to solve this asteroid situation."

"I have an idea," I said. "I wouldn't blow it up, I'd try to land it."

"I'm listening," he said.

"It'll be expensive," I said.

"Too expensive for a couple of zillionaires like us?" he said, smiling.

"Never," I said. "Have you ever heard of graphene?"

CHAPTER 6

The Asteroid Net

Of course Sir Robert had heard of graphene. It's only the most exciting new material on the planet. It's super thin and light, but graphene is also the strongest material known to man.

A few years ago, two scientists won the Nobel Prize for their work with graphene. They said it's so strong that a piece of graphene as thin as plastic wrap is strong enough to hold an elephant!

"We've worked a little with graphene at my facility. An incredible material," Sir Robert said.

"Is it as amazing as people say?" I asked.

"It's flexible, incredibly strong, and can conduct electricity," he said. "It's a miracle material."

Dad and I knew all about graphene. We'd read articles and watched a lot of videos on it. Still, we'd never actually seen it in person.

"Do you have graphene at your facility now?" Dad asked.

"We do," Sir Robert replied. "We plan to use it a great deal in the future, in everything from cell phones to airplanes. But the technology isn't very advanced yet."

"Do you think a giant sheet of it would be strong enough to catch an asteroid?" I asked.

"It's definitely strong enough to catch the asteroid without breaking," he said. "But it would be almost impossible to predict where the asteroid will impact earth. The odds of placing the graphene mesh in the right place is a million-to-one shot."

"I'm not talking about catching the asteroid on Earth," I explained. "I'm talking about catching it in space before it enters the atmosphere. You could use one of your spaceships to get the mesh up there."

Sir Robert stood up and walked over to a large thin computer screen on the wall. He clicked the controls a few times and opened what looked like an animation program. "Benji, come over here," he said. "Let's see if we can't get a sense of exactly what you're talking about."

Dad and I walked over to the screen.

"Tell it what you're thinking," said Sir Robert. "The program will create a visual model."

"You're kidding!" I exclaimed.

"You're not the only person capable of creating a cool computer program, Benji," he said. "If you describe your idea to this program, it will show us what the concept will look like. Give it a go."

"Okay." I had the idea formed in my head, but it was tricky explaining it to the computer program clearly enough so it could create a visual model for us. "We launch a rocket into space containing a graphene mesh long enough and wide enough to catch the asteroid," I began.

The screen immediately displayed an animation of a rocket deploying a long thin sheet in space.

I continued. "Four other rockets would then attach themselves to each corner of the sheet. These rockets would be able to hover in space, holding each corner of the sheet in place to capture the asteroid as it zooms toward Earth."

The high-tech machine took a few seconds, but the screen created an animation similar to the images I had imagined.

"This program is absolutely amazing!" I said.

"Much cooler than a turkey sandwich?" Sir Robert joked.

"Let's hear the rest of your idea, Benji," Dad said. "Don't lose your concentration."

"Well, when the asteroid makes contact with the mesh, the four rockets will fire," I said. "This would allow us to remotely lower the asteroid to Earth safely."

I couldn't believe that in only a few minutes the program managed to create what I was seeing in my mind. I had worried that the plan was a little far-fetched, but seeing it there on the screen, I felt it was possible.

"Begin production of materials," Sir Robert told the program.

"What will that do?" I asked.

"It will send the plans to my team, and they can get to work on it right away."

"That's astonishing," Dad said.

"It's technology, Mr. Franklin."

"I love it," I said.

"You haven't seen anything yet," Sir Robert said.

$ $ $

We touched down about three hours later at his facility in the desert. The place looked like a scene from *Star Wars*. There were several buildings built around what looked like a futuristic airport.

People worked busily everywhere I looked.

He had more jets, race cars, and rockets than I could have imagined. Many of them looked like rockets that had been used a long time ago. "I'm a bit of a collector," he said.

The luxury aircraft came to a stop, and we climbed out and onto the runway. He and Dad talked about the early days of aviation as he gave us a tour of his facility. I could tell Dad was having the time of his life. As the sun was setting Sir Robert said, "I'd like to show you gentlemen my most prized project. Follow me."

We walked to a large building on the far side of the runway. It was buzzing with activity. There were people in bright red suits assembling what looked like spacecraft.

"This is the future, Benji," said Sir Robert. "You're looking at my prize possession. It's the next step in aviation and the craft that will lead humanity into space in large numbers."

I couldn't believe what I was seeing. It was the most advanced rocket ship I'd ever seen, and I'd seen them all online before.

"This is a top secret machine," he continued. "Every part you see is made right here at the space center. I don't take any chances on getting a poor product or on other people learning what I'm up to. I hope I can count on you two to help keep my secret."

"Of course," Dad said.

"I'm just trying to figure out what it can do," I said, looking at the scene in front of me. This wasn't a sci-fi movie. This was the real deal!

"These are low-orbit ships," explained Sir Robert. "Their missions will be programmed ahead of time and no pilots are needed. All you do is open the door, get in, and off you go into the great beyond. Space tourists will get into low orbit, take a few pictures, shoot some video, and basically have the time of their lives."

"It's the coolest idea I've ever heard!" I said.

"We have several ships completed and ready to go. I was just waiting for the right time to test them. We'll use your asteroid plan as the reason to launch them into space."

CHAPTER 7
Suit Up!

That night, Mom called to see how things were going and check if I'd be going to school the next day. Dad told her that the things I was experiencing were too extraordinary to miss and I would probably be out for a few days.

After dinner, one of Sir Robert's assistants showed Dad and me to a small building at the edge of the airport. "You gentlemen will be staying here for the next few days, so make yourselves comfortable," he said. "Please let me know if you need anything."

He gave us each a laptop that accessed my data from Dad's satellite and gave us access to all of Sir Robert's data, too. His satellites were so much more advanced than the one Dad launched. They even had live video feeds from space.

Dad and I were up half the night checking out the satellite data. We must have fallen asleep really late because the next thing I knew, it was morning. I was drooling on the couch and Dad was snoring on the floor.

There was a knock at the front door. It was Sir Robert. He came in and sat next to me on the couch. "I see that you two are settling in."

"We spent most of the night exploring your satellites," Dad said. "They're really fantastic!"

"That's kind of you to say, but I'm just as amazed that you got something up into orbit that functions as a satellite using scrap parts," he said to Dad.

"You haven't seen our property," I said. "It's not your average scrap heap. It's like a storage yard full of everything you can imagine. Dad's been messing around with mechanical things for so long he can build anything."

"I'm just a hobby builder," Dad said.

"My own father was the same way," Dad added. "One time he built me a hovercraft out of a wading pool, a microwave oven, and an electric toothbrush."

"That's absolutely amazing!" Sir Robert said.

"Yeah," said Dad. "It didn't go very far, but I had the cleanest teeth in the state."

"I grew up in private schools full of nannies and tutors," Sir Robert said. "I've always been book smart, but I've never been a do-it-yourself-er. It's good for me to spend this time with you two. You're true inventors in the purest sense."

"And *you're* a super inventor," I told him. "This place is like Disneyland."

"I'm happy to share it with you," he replied, smiling. "We have a busy day planned, but I thought we could have a little fun before we rolled up our sleeves and got to work today."

"Can we fly in one of your ships?" I asked.

"There's no better time than the present."

The ship he showed us could carry two to four passengers. Sir Robert pressed a button on the outside of the ship and three seats popped up. They were large, comfortable-looking and sat next to each other in an arc.

The ship was like a large toy. It reminded me of a WaveRunner, but about three times the size. It had small wings on each side. It looked like it could be part of a ride at an amusement park. I couldn't believe this little thing would be able to carry us into outer space.

"Can it really take us into outer orbit?" I asked.

"It's more than capable. In fact, I think you'll be surprised at how easily the Day Tripper can take us on a round-trip. Are you gents ready for your first taste of space?"

Dad looked like he was about to pop with excitement. If he were a kid he'd be jumping up and down. "I'm ready," Dad said. "I've been ready for this moment since I was a kid."

"Me too," I said sarcastically.

"Benji, when your father and I were children people thought that we'd be able to visit space in our lifetime. But technology didn't deliver it fast enough for me. That's why I decided to create the technology I wanted on my own terms."

"Have you been up before?" I asked.

"This will be my tenth trip up. Only a handful

of people have been up so far. I'm proud to inform you that you'll be the first, uh, non-adult I put into space."

A man rolled up to us with a cart containing three folded-up space suits. "Here are the suits you requested, Sir Robert."

"Thank you, Arthur. We'll be off in about ten minutes. Please alert the team and the tower."

"Will do, sir."

Before I knew it, Dad was seated on the floor and had his suit half on. "Well, I'm thrilled to see you're so excited," Mr. Dransling said. "Let's suit up and get up there!"

Moments later, we were seated in the ship. It really did feel like an amusement park ride. When the engine turned on, it wasn't as loud as I'd expected.

I sat in the middle seat between Dad and Sir Robert. The control panel was really simple. I'd expected it to be full of gadgets and gizmos, but it wasn't. There were cameras showing us a view of the rear and each side of the craft. There was a touch screen in front of each seat giving data such as time, temperature, speed, and so on.

There were several interactive touch tabs: tower comm, video, e-mail, notes, music, and GPS.

That was it. The inside of the ship was simple, clean, and really modern. There was even a drink holder. I wondered if it really kept the drinks in the holder or they simply flew around the ship once it reached zero gravity.

Ah, zero G!! I'd always wanted to go to space, and I'm sure the view is amazing, but the real reason I'd always wanted to go to space was to experience weightlessness.

"Sir Robert, will we be able to experience zero gravity in the ship?" I asked.

"Of course!" he said. "What would a trip to outer space be without experiencing zero G?"

"But, the cockpit ceiling is so low and the area we're sitting in is so tight," Dad said. "I don't understand."

"Trust me. You'll experience zero gravity."

We all buckled in and the ship pulled slowly out of the hangar.

It was a perfect day; there wasn't a cloud in the sky. We rolled along the runway, picking up speed. In twenty seconds, the front tipped up and the ship took flight. It was amazing how safe I felt.

We slowly gained altitude. Before I knew it, we were above the clouds. "How are you guys feeling?" Sir Robert asked.

"Fantastic," I said. "I can't believe we don't need helmets or anything."

"I'm so used to seeing astronauts in heavy gear," Dad added.

"That was one of my main goals with this little ship," said Sir Robert. "I wanted the passengers to feel like they were in a car."

"Or an X-wing fighter!" I said.

"Go ahead and recline if you'd like. The button is on the side of your seat. When we get into outer orbit you may want to lay your seat back completely to get a better look at the stars."

"I'm fine," I said feeling my first bit of nervousness. I didn't want to admit that I was worried, but all of a sudden I was getting more and more nervous by the minute.

The numbers showing our altitude were climbing so fast I couldn't read them and the speed was picking up pretty dramatically. We were climbing quickly. I knew that in a matter of minutes we'd either be in outer space or in a million pieces!

I thought about Mom and how she'd be worried out of her mind if she knew what Dad and I were doing. "Can I call my mom once we're out of Earth's orbit?" I asked.

"Of course. You can call her whenever you like," Sir Robert said. I relaxed a little and couldn't wait to get high enough to see Earth as a blue ball floating in space.

The ship climbed and climbed until I could feel a difference. The engine cut off and the ship seemed to float.

"Did you know that once you've reached an altitude of 50 miles above the planet you are, by definition, an astronaut?" Sir Robert asked.

I looked at the touch screen and we were at 62 miles and counting.

"Welcome to space, gentlemen," he said.

It was such a strange sensation looking back on the planet. It was just like I'd seen it in videos and pictures, but it was real.

Dad literally had a tear in his eye.

For a split second, I felt like I might cry (or throw up!). It was overwhelming.

I was in outer space!

CHAPTER 8
Zero Gravity

"Hi, Mom, I'm in space. What are you doing?"

"What do you mean you're in space? Where's your father?" she asked.

"I'm right here," Dad said leaning over so she could see his face.

"You're kidding, right?"

"I'm happy to report, madam, that your two fellows are officially astronauts and are safely orbiting the blue marble as we speak."

"What are you doing in space!"

"It's fine, Mom. It's the most amazing thing I've ever seen. Sir Robert's ship is so comfortable you wouldn't even believe it's a spaceship."

"I wish you would have called to let me know before deciding to blast off."

"It all happened so fast," Dad said. "It seemed like the opportunity of a lifetime."

"I'll have them safely back on the ground in less than twenty minutes, Mum."

I thought it was a little odd that he called Mom, Mum. I could tell by the look on her face that she didn't like it. "All right, but you call me the second you're back on Earth!" Mom insisted.

"Roger that," I said, hanging up.

"You were wondering about zero gravity," Sir Robert reminded me. "Press the button on your touch pad."

A clickable button appeared on my touch pad that read Zero Gravity. I pressed the button and immediately the glass cover above our heads rose up. It stretched up about fifteen feet before stopping.

Sir Robert unclicked his harness and rolled forward into zero gravity. "Feel free to unbuckle when you're ready."

"Let's go!" Dad said enthusiastically.

I clicked the button on my harness and immediately felt weightless. Rather than stay in my seat like I would have on Earth, I gently floated out. I reached out to grab something to balance myself and ended up grabbing Dad's ankle. Sir Robert was already about five feet above us and doing somersaults. I noticed a pen fall out of his pocket and float in the air near him.

I pushed off Dad's ankle and propelled up toward the ceiling of the ship. I tucked my knees up to my chest and rotated over in a flip. "This is the absolute best thing ever! We've got to get Mom up here one day," I said.

"You can e-mail her a video of the entire flight. The ship records everything," Sir Robert said.

"Can I have a copy?" I asked.

"If your plan to capture the asteroid works, you can have more than that," he said.

For the first time since I climbed into the ship, I thought about the real reason we'd come to the desert. We were there to help capture an asteroid. It was time to return to Earth and get to work. Sir Robert clicked a button and the ceiling started lowering back to its original size. We all buckled back in and began our descent to Earth. I took one last look at the planet from space.

"Soak it up, Benji," Dad said. "You may never get an opportunity to visit space again."

"I'm quite certain this is the first of many space flights for young Master Franklin," Sir Robert said.

"I hope you're right," I said.

"Trust me," he said. "You'll be back."

CHAPTER 9

Nice Catch!

It was a good thing that we got an early start on all the preparations because the asteroid was traveling faster than we originally realized. After about a week of people working around the clock at the facility we were ready to put my plan into motion. Dad and I stayed in New Mexico the whole week. Since we were working, Mom decided to stay and help out in Shiny Desert until we were ready to head home.

Dad, Sir Robert, and I went back into space in one of his ships before the rockets were launched. One of his teams stayed at the facility and another prepared the landing spot for the asteroid. Once we were in space Sir Robert handed me the digital screen that controlled the rockets. "The moment of truth has arrived, Benji."

I took a deep breath. There was so much adrenaline rushing through my body I felt like I might burst. "What if this doesn't work?" I asked.

"What if it does?" he said.

"It will be the most amazing thing ever," I said.

"Then let's do the most amazing thing ever!"

Dad patted me on the back. "Let's do it. It's time to put things in motion."

On my screen I had a view of the asteroid. It was approaching exactly as we'd planned. I clicked the button to launch the first four rockets. The video from the ground showed all four firing and launching. I waited a few seconds and clicked to launch the fifth rocket containing the graphene mesh. It blasted off exactly as planned.

"Phase one complete," Sir Robert said.

We watched the video screens from each rocket and the coordinates of where they were located. Within minutes, they were in place.

They were each programmed to carry out the mission, but if anything went wrong, I had the ability to override the program from our ship.

The fifth rocket released the graphene mesh and cut its engines as planned. The other four maneuvered into position. Each one docked into a corner of the mesh, spreading it out like a gigantic space web. We zoomed closer in our ship for a visual inspection of the setup. I felt like I was dreaming. There I was in space about to catch an asteroid!

"Is this really happening?" I asked Dad as we circled the mesh.

"It is really happening," Dad said. "Don't ask me how, but it's happening!"

"We better move to a safer distance," Sir Robert said. "This is all going to happen very fast."

We traveled for a while until we all agreed we were safely away from the asteroid. We tracked its every move on the video screen.

It was moving so fast I started to feel concerned that it would destroy the mesh and crash to Earth. I held my breath for what seemed like forever as it approached.

Closer...closer...

It made a direct hit with the center of the mesh, which ignited all four rockets. The force of the rockets pulled in the opposite direction that the asteroid was traveling. We worried that the force of the asteroid would tear the mesh away from the rockets, but the graphene was strong enough to hold on. It stretched out a bunch, and kept stretching!

The force of the rockets slowed the asteroid dramatically. The force of the asteroid's speed and the force of the rockets created an epic battle of tug-of-war. Which would win?

Within a few minutes it was over and the asteroid was gliding safely under the control of the rockets. "Phase two complete," Sir Robert said sounding relieved.

Dad didn't say a word. He was sweating pretty heavily. I noticed that his fingers were crossed. "Are you all right, Dad?" I asked.

"About as good as I can be under the circumstances."

Phase three of the plan was the part I was looking forward to most. The rockets carefully guided the asteroid down toward Earth. We followed behind. We were close enough to watch it with our own eyes. The asteroid was far more massive than I'd imagined. It was like a floating mountain.

I couldn't believe how well the rockets were working. At the pace they were going we'd be on the surface in a matter of minutes.

"You should probably call Mom," Dad said.

He was right.

I clicked the screen and dialed Mom. Her face appeared on the screen. "Hi, Mom! What are you doing?"

"I'm working. We just got back to Shiny Desert a little while ago. I made another run back to the farm to pick up more supplies for the town."

"Great! Do me a favor. Head outside and look up in the sky."

"Benji, I'm pretty busy. We've got a load of supplies that we need to organize."

"Trust me. I'll see you in a few minutes." Then I hung up.

"Phase four coming up," Dad said.

"Phase four on the way," I said. We were getting low enough that I could see the ground. We were under the clouds. Things were coming into view.

"There," Dad said. "There's Mom's truck."

I saw the truck and spotted Mom. She had walked out of a building and was looking up at us. I could only imagine what was going through her mind gazing up at a massive asteroid supported by four rockets.

People from the nearby town were pouring out of the buildings too. There was a real commotion.

The rockets safely landed the asteroid on the exact coordinates we'd programmed. It was the perfect spot just outside the town.

The ground vibrated when the space rock made contact. Sir Robert landed our ship near the asteroid and Mom ran over to meet us.

CHAPTER 10
Bright Future

By the time the team sprayed down the asteroid with water and it cooled to a safe level, hundreds of people had lined up for a look. Sir Robert's team handed him a microphone.

"Citizens of Shiny Desert," he began. "We at Dransling Industries realize that you've fallen on hard times. You're a hard-working community. You don't deserve the misfortune that fell upon you when Techron left you without jobs. I wasn't familiar with your story until a young friend of mine brought it to my attention. Through a series of miraculous events we've managed to save the planet from a deadly asteroid *and* your town all at once.

"Please accept this asteroid as a gift. It should provide adequate income as a tourist destination for many years to come."

"Additionally," said the billionaire. "I plan to move a portion of my business here to your town. I'm building my space tourism business, and I'm opening an assembly plant right here in Shiny Desert. Construction of the new plant will begin as soon as possible and we will begin hiring tomorrow. We look forward to a bright future together!"

The crowd cheered.

"This was all your idea, wasn't it?" Mom asked. "I don't know what to say. Benji, you managed to solve the town's problems and save the planet in one swoop. You're my very own pint-sized hero!"

I was kind of overwhelmed by it all. It had been a crazy couple of weeks. I knew my life would never be the same again, but I also knew I wanted to try to keep from changing as much as I could.

That's when I heard Sir Robert say, "Folks, I can't stand up here and take all the credit for today. There's a young man who was the brains behind this whole thing. He's here somewhere…"

"He's talking about you, Benji," Mom said. "Get ready to go up on the stage."

I took Mom by the hand and quickly led her out of the crowd. "What are we doing?" Mom asked.

"The hero never sticks around for a thank-you," I reminded her. "Besides, I have something I want to show you."

I led Mom over to the ship. "Get a load of this!" I exclaimed.

"Benji, this is very pretty, but we should be getting back."

"I'd rather show you something else," I said.

Dad ran up to us. "I lost you guys back there. Benji, Sir Robert is looking for you."

"Let him take the credit. I'd rather take Mom for a spin."

"Great idea," Dad said. He opened the door. "After you, my dear."

"Where are we going?" Mom asked.

"Trust me," I said. We all climbed in. I called Sir Robert's phone. His face appeared on the screen. "Benji, where are you? These people want to thank you."

"You enjoy it. I'm going to take my Mom for a spin if that's all right with you."

"By all means. Just don't forget to swing by and pick me up when you're done."

"Will do," I said. I hung up and told Mom to get ready.

"Benji, do you know how to control this thing?"

"I don't need to. It's already programmed."

"Programmed to go where?"

"To space," I said, pressing the launch button. The ship lifted off the ground. Mom screamed and grabbed onto Dad.

"Will I like it?" she asked, looking terrified.

"You'll love it," I said, and the ship bolted up toward outer space.

Mom let out another scream, and then she said, "Benji, you're too much! What on Earth are you going to accomplish next!"

"I have no idea," I said. "But I can't wait to find out!"

NEO
(near earth object)

NOTICE OF PAYMENT

FROM:
NEO (Near Earth Object)

TO:
Benjamin "Benji" Franklin

ITEM:	QUANTITY:	AMOUNT:
Liquid Fueled Rockets	5	$8,000,000
Graphene Sheeting	160,000 Feet	$1,500,000
Liquid Jet Fuel	1	$235,000
Cash Registers	2	$450
1 Story Building	1	$654,550

TOTAL COST: $10,390,000

PAYMENT DUE UPON RECEIPT

PAID!

Cha-Ching!!

RAYMOND BEAN

Raymond Bean is the best-selling author of the Sweet Farts and School Is A Nightmare series. His books have ranked #1 in Children's Humor, Humorous Series, and Fantasy and Adventure categories. He writes for kids that claim they don't like reading.

Mr. Bean is a fourth grade teacher with fifteen years of classroom experience. He lives with his wife and two children in New York.

Glossary

access (AK-ses)—a way to enter, or an approach to a place

adequate (AD-i-kwit)—just enough, or good enough

adrenaline (uh-DREN-uh-lin)—a chemical that your body produces when you need more energy or when you sense danger

chauffer (SHOH-fur)—a person who is hired to drive a car for somebody else

collision (kuh-LIZH-uhn)—a crash in which two or more objects hit each other

coordinates (koh-OR-duh-nits)—numbers used to show the position of a point on a map, graph, or line

discretion (dis-KREH-shuhn)—individual choice or judgment

remotely (ri-MOHT-lee)—from far away in space or time

scenarios (suh-NAIR-ee-ohs)—outlines of series of events that might happen in particular situations

skeptical (SKEP-ti-kuhl)—doubting that something is really true

Million-Dollar Questions

1. Benji misses a lot of school to help Sir Robert. Do you think it was worth it? Is there a way that Benji could have kept his commitment to school AND solved the asteroid problem?

2. Benji comes up with several ideas to save Earth from the asteroid headed toward it. Do you think he chose the best solution? Come up with some other solutions, and decide which one you think would work best if an asteroid really was about to hit Earth.

3. Do you think that Sir Robert could have come up with a solution to stop the asteroid from hitting Earth on his own? Why do you think he asked for Benji's help?

4. Identify a problem that you've noticed in your home or classroom. Maybe your doorbell at home doesn't work, or one of your classmates always mistakes your locker for hers. Now think like Benji! What can you do to solve this problem? What will you need?

5. Benji knows his mom is trying to help out the town of Shiny Desert, so he lands the asteroid there so that it can be utilized as a tourist attraction and bring money to the town. Write a chapter that continues the story after the end of this book. What happens in Shiny Desert? Does Benji's plan work?

6. When they land the asteroid successfully, Benji doesn't want the attention of the crowd. Write about a time when you succeeded at something. Were you embarassed by the attention it brought you?

1,000,000,000,000,000,000,000,000

BENJI FRANKLIN

KID ZILLIONAIRE

The fun doesn't stop here!

Discover more at...
www.**CAPSTONEKIDS**.com

Find cool websites and more books like this one at www.Facthound.com. Just type in the BOOK ID: 9781434264183 and you're ready to go!